MICE ON ICE

by **Eleanor May** • Illustrated by **Deborah Melmon**

THE KANE PRESS / NEW YORK

For Brady and Logan, the nicest mice on ice—E.M.

For Hayley and Adi—D.M.

Library of Congress Cataloging-in-Publication Data

May, Eleanor.
Mice on ice / by Eleanor May ; illustrated by Deborah Melmon.
    p. cm. — (Mouse math)
    "With fun activities!"
Summary: Albert joins his sister and friends mice skating on the frozen pond, but when he tries to
make shapes as they do, he runs into some problems.
ISBN 978-1-57565-527-7 (library reinforced binding : alk. paper) — ISBN 978-1-57565-528-4 (pbk. :
alk. paper) — ISBN 978-1-57565-529-1 (e-book)
    [1. Mice—Fiction. 2. Shape—Fiction. 3. Ice skating—Fiction.] I. Melmon, Deborah, ill. II. Title.
PZ7.M4513Mic 2013
[E]—dc23   2012029505

1 3 5 7 9 10 8 6 4 2

First published in the United States of America in 2013 by Kane Press, Inc.
Printed in the United States of America
WOZ0113

Book Design: Edward Miller

Mouse Math is a trademark of Kane Press, Inc.

Visit us online at **www.kanepress.com**

 Like us on Facebook
facebook.com/kanepress

 Follow us on Twitter
@KanePress

Dear Parent/Educator,

"I can't do math." Every child (or grownup!) who says these words has at some point along the way felt intimidated by math. For young children who are just being introduced to the subject, we wanted to create a world in which math was not simply numbers on a page, but a part of life—an adventure!

Enter Albert and Wanda, two little mice who live in the walls of a People House. Children will be swept along with this irrepressible duo and their merry band of friends as they tackle mouse-sized problems and dilemmas. (And sometimes *cat-sized* problems and dilemmas!)

Each book in the MOUSE MATH™ series provides a fresh take on a basic math concept. The mice discover solutions as they, for instance, use position words while teaching a pet snail to do tricks or count the alarmingly large number of friends they've invited over on a rainy day—and, lo and behold, they are doing math!

Math educators who specialize in early childhood learning used their expertise to make sure each title would be as helpful as possible to young kids—and to their parents and teachers. Fun activities at the end of the books and on our website encourage children to think and talk about math in ways that will make each concept clear and memorable.

As with our award-winning Math Matters® series, our aim is to captivate children's imaginations by drawing them into the story, and so into the math at the heart of each adventure. It is our hope that kids will want to hear and read the MOUSE MATH stories again and again and that, as they grow up, they will approach math with enthusiasm and see it as an invaluable tool for navigating the world they live in.

Sincerely,

Joanne Kane

Joanne E. Kane
Publisher

"The puddle's frozen!" Albert said.
"We can go mice skating!"

Albert and his sister, Wanda, hurried to get ready.

"Can you help me zip up?" Albert asked Wanda.

"Albert, what in the world are you wearing?"
Wanda asked.

"Pillows!" Albert said. "To make it softer
when I—OOF!"

Wanda helped Albert up. "Are you okay?"

"I'm fine!" he said. "The pillows worked!"

6

Outside, they saw their friends Leo and Lucy.
Leo waved. "We're skating shapes!"

"Shapes?" Albert asked.

Lucy pointed. "See? The Mousely triplets are making a **triangle**."

"A triangle is perfect for the triplets!" Wanda said. "Each triplet gets to skate one of the triangle's three sides."

triangle

"I can do a triangle!" Albert said. "Watch!"
He skated one side . . .

Then another side . . .

Then . . .

CRASH.

"Albert, a triangle has *three* sides," Lucy said. "Not two."

Albert looked up at them. "I guess I missed the turn."

"I have an idea!" Leo said.
"There are four of us. A **square** has four equal sides.
We can each skate one straight line and make a square."

square

They took their places.

"Don't forget," Lucy told Albert.

"When you get to the end of your side, STOP."

"Ready. Set. Go!"
Lucy skated a straight line to Leo.
Leo skated a straight line to Wanda.

Wanda skated a straight line to Albert.

Albert wiggled.

Then he wobbled.

Then he— **"WHOOPS!"**

Wanda helped Albert up.

"Albert, a square has four STRAIGHT sides," Lucy said.

Albert looked at their shape.
"My side isn't so straight," he admitted.
"But I stopped at the end!"

Wanda bought Albert a cup of hot chocolate.
"Maybe you'd do better with a **circle**," Wanda said.
"A circle doesn't have any straight lines."

Wanda showed Albert how to skate in a circle.

"Now you try!"
she said.

circle

Albert stood up.

Albert sat down.

Wanda said, "Let's hold paws and skate together."

Albert and Wanda skated off.

"That's good!" Wanda said. "You're doing great!"

"Keep turning!" Wanda said. "Turn, Albert! TURN!"

Albert looked at the ice.

"That's not a very good circle, is it?"

"No," Wanda agreed. . . .

"But it's an excellent **oval**!" she finished with a smile.

"Wow!" Albert said. "We made an oval!
Wait till Leo sees this!"

oval

Albert zoomed off.
He was going *very* fast.

Wanda called after him. "Albert, slow down!"

Albert called back, "I CAN'T!"

Albert whizzed straight toward Leo.
"Yikes!" Leo flung up his paws and fell over.

"Sorry!" Albert cried, making a sharp turn just in time.

"Whew!" he gasped.
"That was close!"

"EEEEK!"
the Mousely triplets
squeaked.

"Sorry!" Albert called as he made another sharp turn.

"ALBERT!" Lucy shouted.

"Oops!" Albert veered again.

"Sorry, Lucy! I'll buy you another hot cho—

AAAAAAAAAAAAAAHHHHH!"

"Wanda!" Albert gasped. "Are you okay?"

Wanda laughed. "I'm fine! The pillows worked!"

"And look—you made a **rectangle**!" she said. "All by yourself!"

"I did?" Albert said. "Wow! Wait till Leo sees this!"

rectangle

Albert zoomed off again.

Wanda put a paw over her eyes.
"Next time, we'd better bring
pillows for EVERYONE!"

▲ 2 FUN ACTIVITIES ❸ 4

Mice on Ice supports children's understanding of **two-dimensional shapes**, an important topic in early math learning. Use the activities below to extend the math topic and to reinforce children's early reading skills.

🐭 ENGAGE

Remind children that the cover of a book can tell them a lot about the story inside.

▶ Invite children to look at the illustration as you read the title aloud. Ask: *What do you think this story is about? What are the mice doing? Can you spot anything in the ice?* (You may wish to record children's responses and refer back to them at the end of the story.)

🐭 LOOK BACK

▶ Before reading the story aloud, ask children if they have ever been ice skating. If so, encourage them to talk about their experience. What was it like? Were they afraid? Was it easy? What was the most difficult part of skating?

▶ After reading the story, have children look back at page 4. Ask: *How does Albert know that he and Wanda can go ice skating? Look at pages 5 and 6. Why do you think Albert is wearing pillows? Do they help? How do you know?*

▶ Look at page 7. Ask: *What are the other mice doing when Albert and Wanda arrive? Do you think the other mice are good skaters? What makes you think so?*

▶ Turn to page 22. Ask: *What shape was Albert trying to make? What shape did he end up making?*

🐭 TRY THIS!

▶ Pull pre-cut shapes out of a bag and ask the children to identify them. Shapes should include a triangle, square, circle, oval, and rectangle. (If you wish, you may print out a reference page of shapes for each child from www.kanepress.com/mousemath-2d.html.)

▶ On three separate pieces of paper, draw the numbers 3, 4, and 4 again. Now place the triangle, square, and rectangle cutouts back into the bag. Remove the shapes one at a time, and ask children to match a numeral to each shape; the numeral should indicate how many sides the shape has. Explain that both the square and the rectangle have four sides, but the square's four sides are equal in length.

▶ As an added challenge, you may wish to draw a pentagon (5 sides), a hexagon (6 sides), and an octagon (8 sides) on the board. Invite children to describe each shape. Pay special attention to the number of sides, and count them aloud with the children. Make cutouts of these shapes and add them to the bag. Then repeat the first activity.

▶ **Bonus:** Give children pre-cut strips of paper and ask them to form different shapes using one strip for each side. First give them only three strips, then four, then five, etc. See if they can name their shapes. Can they form a circle with the strips? Why not? Is there something they could use to form a circle? (Hint: a piece of string.)

🐭 THINK!

▶ Encourage children to look back in the story and find all the shapes that Albert and his friends made in the ice. Record children's findings on the board or on a large sheet of paper. You may wish to ask for volunteers to draw each shape and write the word for that shape underneath it.

▶ Now it's time to go *rice skating*! Give a small cookie tray to each child or pair of children. Pour enough rice on the tray to cover its surface. Have children use their index fingers to draw (or take turns drawing) all the different shapes found in the story. They may refer to the shapes on the board for help.

◆ **FOR MORE ACTIVITIES** ◆

visit www.kanepress.com/mousemath-activities.html